I Want My Potty

First published in Great Britain by Andersen Press Ltd in 1986
First published in Picture Lions in 1987
This edition published in 1992

10 9 8 7 6 5

Picture Lions is an imprint of the Children's Division,
part of HarperCollins Publishers Limited,
77-85 Fulham Palace Road, Hammersmith,
London W6 8JB

PRINTED IN CHINA

I Want My Potty

Tony Ross

PictureLions

An Imprint of HarperCollins*Publishers*

"Nappies are YUUECH!" said the little princess.
"There MUST be something better!"

"The potty's the place," said the queen.

At first the little princess thought the potty was
worse.

"THE POTTY'S THE PLACE!" said the queen.

So . . . the little princess had to learn.

Sometimes the little princess was a long way from the potty when she needed it most.

Sometimes the little princess played tricks on the potty . . .

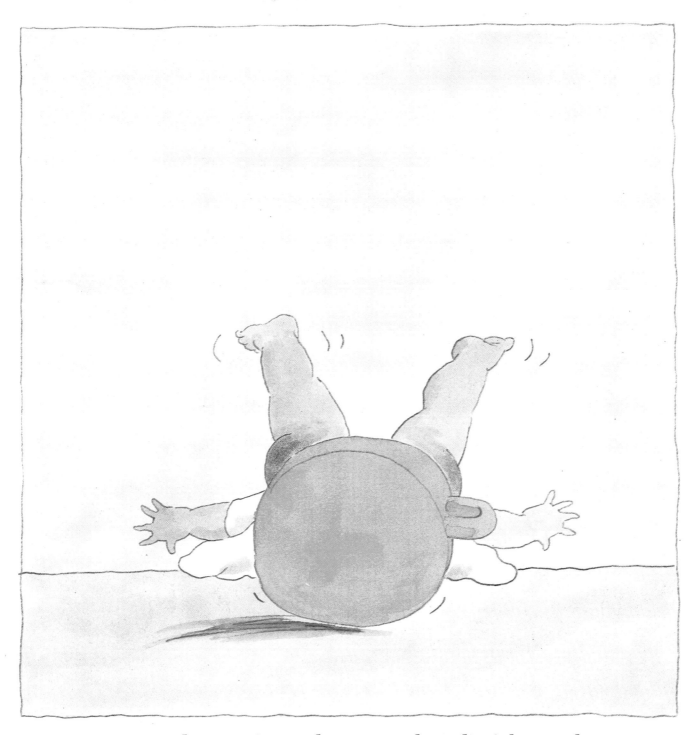

. . . and sometimes the potty played tricks on the little princess.

Soon the potty was fun

and the little princess loved it.

Everybody said the little princess was clever and
would grow up to be a wonderful queen.

"The potty's the place!" said the little princess proudly.

One day the little princess was playing at the top of
the castle . . . when . . .

"I WANT MY POTTY!" she cried.

"She wants her potty," cried the maid.

"She wants her potty," cried the king.

"She wants her potty," cried the cook.

"She wants her potty," cried the gardener.

"She wants her potty," cried the general.

"I know where it is," cried the admiral.

So the potty was taken as quickly as possible

to the little princess . . . just

. . . a little too late.

Tony Ross was born in London in 1938. His dream was to work with horses but instead he went to art college in Liverpool. Since then, Tony has worked as an art director at an advertising agency, a graphic designer, a cartoonist, a teacher and a film maker – as well as illustrating over 250 books! Tony and his wife Zoe live in Macclesfield, Cheshire and have four children.

Picture Lions by Tony Ross
I WANT TO BE – the hilarious sequel to *I Want My Potty*
SUPER DOOPER JEZEBEL
THE KNIGHT WHO WAS AFRAID OF THE DARK
JENNA AND THE TROUBLE MAKER
RECKLESS RUBY

Here are some more Picture Lions

for you to enjoy.